flying lessons

ALSO BY NAVA SEMEL

Becoming Gershona

flying lessons

BY NAVA SEMEL

TRANSLATED BY HILLEL HALKIN

SIMON & SCHUSTER BOOKS FOR YOUNG READERS

SIMON & SCHUSTER BOOKS FOR YOUNG READERS

An imprint of Simon & Schuster Children's Publishing Division

1230 Avenue of the Americas, New York, New York 10020

First published in Israel as *Maurice Chaviv'el Melamed La'oof*

by Am Oved Publishers Ltd, 1990.

First American Edition, 1995

SIMON & SCHUSTER BOOKS FOR YOUNG READERS is a trademark of Simon & Schuster.

Designed by Paul Zakris

The text of this book is set in 13-point Perpetua

Manufactured in the United States of America

First edition

10 9 8 7 6 5 4 3 2 1

Library of Congress Cataloging-in-Publication Data

Semel, Nava.

   [Morris Haviv'el melamed la-'uf. English]

   Flying Lessons / by Nava Semel ; translated by Hillel Halkin

     p.   cm.

   Summary: Living in a village in Israel where her father grows oranges, a

motherless girl befriends a sensitive shoemaker from Djerba from whom she hopes to

learn how to fly.

   ISBN 0-689-80161-0

   1. Jews—Israel—Juvenile fiction. [1. Jews—Israel—Fiction. 2. Israel—

Fiction. 3. Holocaust survivors—Fiction] I. Halkin, Hillel, 1939-

II. Title.

PZ7.S4657F1   1995   [Fic]—dc20   95-1755   CIP   AC

To Rivka Semel, my late mother-in-law,
who spent most of her life among the citruses
—NS

f l y i n g
l e s s o n s

one

Ever since I could remember, we had used the tall wardrobe for storing summer clothes in winter and winter clothes in summer. I don't remember who decided on it. Maybe it was my mother. Each time the seasons changed, we staged the same ritual. My father brought the big ladder from the citrus grove and set it by the wardrobe, and I positioned myself below him and carefully handed up to him folded blankets, sweaters, and woolen socks rolled into balls. Sometimes I noticed a stain on something, but I never said anything. My father was pretty good at doing the laundry, and I didn't want to hurt his feelings.

Whenever the summer or the winter ended— I never discovered how he chose the exact day— he announced to me that tomorrow we would put things in the tall wardrobe. The next day he'd climb athletically to the top of his fruit picker's ladder and stand on it perfectly straight with his hair brushing the ceiling. From below

I'd stare at his back, and at his hands stuffing clothing through the black opening. I never got to see what was all the way at the back of the closet. The whole thing lasted only a few minutes. I would stand there obediently, sending up one after another the neat bundles that we had packed the night before like oranges in their crates. It was my only chance to see how many clothes we had (not many) and which dress I hated the most (like the lacy one with the puffed sleeves). What luck that I had gotten through a whole year without having to wear it!

Each time my father turned around to face me, bending slightly and reaching down with outstretched arms, I would stand on tiptoe and give him another bundle.

"You've been biting your nails again," he'd say disappointedly. "What are we going to do with you, Hadara?"

I blushed. It was too late to hide my hands beneath the straight fold of the pink blanket. I tried changing the subject by asking, "Is this how you pick oranges?"

My father laughed and said that sometimes some oranges were too high up to pick.

"What happens to them?"

He shrugged and the ladder swayed a bit, or perhaps I only thought it did. I didn't want him to fall and leave both me and the oranges with no one to look after them. Maybe there was still an orange left on a tree from last winter. If I tried hard enough, maybe I could find one that had been there for so many years that even my mother had seen it.

One day in autumn I wanted to drag the ladder from the grove but could not, because the tangerine harvest had started the same morning and a green chain of fruit ran from the trees to the crates and from there to the truck and the port. So to get close enough to climb on top of the tall wardrobe, I had to stand one chair on another, which was scary and a little dangerous. I knew that my father would never have let me do it. At most I might have talked him into letting me put a chair on the table. My father always knew the right angle to stand a ladder at.

"Keeping your balance," he liked to say, even while rocking me in the hammock in the garden, "is the most important thing of all."

❖   ❖   ❖

I stretched my arms out and back, bent my knees, and pressed my ankles together. The house was empty and quiet. My father had left early. The picking season always excited him. I took a deep breath. I was standing on top of the wardrobe with my head almost touching the ceiling, as ready as could be. Through the window I made out the distant green blotch of our citrus grove. It was too far away for me to hear the shouts or to see my father running from tree to tree, petting the tangerines as though they were children.

I toed the edge of the wardrobe to test its stability and straightened my arms, and I wondered what I'd do with my hands and fingers once I'd leaped. Should I open them like feathers? I had no idea. The distance from the wardrobe to the opposite wall seemed about right for a first try. Not a sound came from the outside. The grove was far away, and I was all alone. Now was the time. I tried convincing myself that I could do it. A clothes wardrobe might not be the best place, but it was the mountain of the house, the highest spot with the deepest and darkest cavern. One day, I thought, I would find out what was really buried back there. Perhaps I would find some clothing of my mother's. But not today.

If only there had been a mirror facing me, I could have had the satisfaction of watching myself in action. I was no longer sure that the wardrobe would be steady enough, but it was too late to back down now. And although I would have liked to open the wardrobe doors and peek inside, I was afraid that turning my head would make me lose the balance that my father thought was so important. I wondered if the clothes were confused. Could the whole winter, they must be asking themselves, already have passed so quickly? I stretched myself and took a deep, deep gulp of air. One. Two. Thr——

If it hadn't been for Monsieur Maurice, who appeared at that very moment, I would have done it. I could almost feel the wardrobe rocking beneath me. From above, Monsieur Maurice looked like a small boy and his voice came from the wrong direction.

"What are you doing? *What* are you doing?"

I was about to fly.

t w o

Monsieur Maurice Havivel was a new neighbor in our village. When all the citrus growers went out to their groves, he would amble over to his shoemaker's shop behind our house. Although my father was a citrus grower too, a year ago he had chosen to move us away from the other growers, into the workers' part of the village. Zussman, who owned the second-largest citrus grove, was so angry at this breach of tradition that he didn't talk to my father all last winter.

Monsieur Maurice Havivel was the one and only shoemaker in our village. Apart from citrus groves, the village had one of everything. There was one photographer, one grocer, one druggist, one doctor, one nurse, and one junk dealer. There was even only one classroom for all of the school-aged children. The only thing there were two of was barbers, one from Poland and one from Turkey. The Polish barber spoke Yiddish with his customers, the Turkish barber, Ladino.

The Turkish barber sang when he worked, and the hair flew in all directions. The Polish barber worked quietly, snipping one hair at a time and sweeping up before his customer had time to remove the white bib from his neck. I knew all this even though I had never been to a barber myself. I had a long braid that my father braided each morning before I went to school, just like a challah bread. I would have liked to have my hair cut, at least once, but my father was dead set against it.

"Your mother had a braid too," he said. I could see that I would never change his mind.

Tova, who owned the notions store at the end of the main street, which was the one and only notions store in the village, said that Monsieur Maurice was the best shoemaker ever to come to Israel, although I think she must have been a bit in love with him. In her store she sold shoelaces, pins, buttons, and needles, and she even had a drawer full of nothing but thimbles. The store had belonged to her parents, and now she was busy looking for a husband, someone who could help out so that she wouldn't have to be on her feet all day long. She told

Monsieur Maurice that he could have all the shoelaces he wanted on credit, but he paid no attention to her compliments and wouldn't accept any gifts from her, not even a little piece of chocolate.

Besides being the one and only shoemaker in our village, he fixed all the shoes of the next village too. Sooner or later any torn sole, worn boot, or buckleless sandal ended up in his shop, because Monsieur Maurice Havivel could make your old shoes look like new.

His shoe shop faced the window of my room. It was a tiny, poorly lit place without even a sign outside. Dozens of pairs of shoes of all shapes and colors lined the shelves: ladies' shoes that had lost their heels waltzing, men's shoes that still had winter mud on them, children's shoes that had played one soccer game too many. Monsieur Maurice allowed me to touch them all as long as I didn't mix them up.

"A pair of shoes must never be separated," he warned me. "The love between two shoes is greater than the love between two people. If one of them gets lost, it's all over with the other."

Monsieur Maurice usually held his hammer

in one hand while stroking the leather of the shoe he was fixing with his other hand, as though it were very ill. The really impressive thing, though, was the row of sharp nails he kept between his teeth. I never understood how he could manage to talk without swallowing them by mistake.

"It wouldn't matter if I did," he said one day. "There was a performer in our circus who swallowed nails like raisins."

I've never seen a circus, I thought to myself. Circuses sometimes came to Tel Aviv, but never to our village. Once, on Purim, a monkey tamer came and tried to make his monkey play the drum, but it ran away to the citrus groves and wasn't found until two days later, after its owner had given up on it; it was stuffing itself with green oranges.

"Everything is possible if you practice," said Monsieur Maurice. "Swallowing nails or flying. If you plan it right, you can get it down pat. So what if it's already been tried? Just because others have given up doesn't mean that you should. Flying isn't all that complicated. Trapeze artists can do it."

He smiled at me mysteriously, as if he were keeping some big secret to himself. Not a nail moved in his mouth.

"In our circus . . . but don't ever tell anyone that I was in a circus—absolutely no one—because if you do . . ."

I was brushing some shoes for him with a stiff-haired brush and was tired. Monsieur Maurice must have been tired too, because he agreed to take a few nails from his mouth and explain how one flies. First, though, he glanced all around to make sure that no one was eavesdropping and that Tova hadn't taken a lunch break and found some excuse to come to his shoe shop. Then he shut the door and continued in a whisper.

"You have to know exactly what you're doing, what part of your body to make use of and when. If birds can do it, why not people? The smaller you are, the lighter you are. And grown-ups have so many worries and troubles that it weighs them down like a sack on their backs."

I listened to every word. Monsieur Maurice slowly took apart a sole, leaving its poor shoe looking naked.

"Are you sure you can put that back together again?"

He didn't answer. I watched him press the pedal of his big sewing machine. I couldn't see any sack on his back. Monsieur Maurice wasn't always a shoemaker, I told myself. Once he was a flier in the circus. He's light and can take to the air, because he has nothing weighing him down. I have to get him to teach me. I'll be the one and only flier in the village.

"Do you think you can put that sole back on without anyone knowing that you did it?" I asked.

"As sure as your name is Hadara," said Monsieur Maurice, and sighed, right into his mouthful of nails.

three

There was a drought that year. The farmers went out to the groves every day to water the thirsty trees. The winter rains hadn't come, and Monsieur Maurice's shelves were full of shoes scratched by dry thorns. Arele Zussman left school before the last bell and hurried off to help his father carry water buckets. The village well was so low that you could see the bottom.

"Don't you want to help your father?" Arele Zussman asked me.

"Do you think I can make it rain?"

Arele gave my braid a tug and went off. It made him flush with anger to be teased that his father's grove was only the second biggest in the village. I never understood why being the best swimmer in the village wasn't enough for him. All the girls at school had a crush on him, even though he had a problem: Arele was a stutterer. But girls didn't interest him. All that did was grafting trees. He was always in the middle of some weird experiment in the shack behind his house, which was the finest house any farmer had. Rina Neumann, one of our classmates, sometimes snuck into his backyard for a look and told the other girls in strictest secrecy what he was up to. The winter that his father hadn't spoken to my father, Arele hadn't spoken to me either. The only time he'd forgotten the family shunning was when once he asked me if we had gotten our shipment of baby lemon trees from Cyprus yet. He had to try to say "Cyprus" three times before he could get the word out. Even though our fathers were feuding, I waited patiently and didn't make fun of him.

Monsieur Maurice's pairs of shoes were the color of dried earth. They stared at me from their shelves like a lot of wrinkled faces.

"They're prematurely old," said Monsieur Maurice, applying another layer of polish to an old pair of work boots. I had tried every trick I knew to get him to teach me. I had been as sweet as pie to him, used my cute-little-baby voice, the one my father hated, and put on my important-lady and even my dangerous-spy look. Nothing had worked.

Monsieur Maurice didn't want to hear of it. He said that he no longer remembered. That the circus belonged to the past and now there was nothing but shoes. And in fact, one pair of fancy slippers had been on his shelf forever. They were the only shoes I wasn't allowed to touch, because—so he said—they were waiting for the lady who owned them to come and ask for their return. I had never seen such special shoes in my life. They were milky white, had a necklace of silver beads around the ankles, and looked too delicate to walk in. If I owned a pair of shoes like that, I thought, I would wear them on my hands like gloves and sleep with them at night.

"Whose shoes are they?"

"Don't ask so many questions. Someone who wants to fly should be thinking of wings, not shoes."

How could I convince him that I was thinking of nothing else all day long? I certainly hoped he didn't think I was thinking of Arele Zussman.

Tova from the notions store didn't like my spending so much time at the shoemaker's. Twice a week she came to cook for us, because cooking wasn't one of my father's specialties. "Why don't you go play with someone your own age?" she grumbled. She didn't know that I had checked out her notions store for silver threads, which it didn't have, though it had enough shoelaces to last the village a hundred years. There were so many that she could have let Monsieur Maurice have all he wanted free of charge.

"Are you planning to take up shoemaking or something? I never saw such a thing. Just you wait until your father finds out!" She shook a red-polished fingernail at me. One of the things I had noticed about her was that she never managed to polish the whole nail.

I pestered Monsieur Maurice every day. The rainless winter was a perfect time for practicing. There wasn't a cloud in the sky, and even the wind seemed asleep. I knew you couldn't learn to fly in the rain. Flocks of birds had arrived to spend the winter in the treetops, but there was no sign of winter itself. One day when the window of our classroom had a few raindrops on it, Arele Zussman jumped to his feet, knocking over a chair, and ran outside.

"Rain!" he yelled. A few minutes later he came back looking shamefaced. The teacher felt so sorry for him that she didn't even punish him.

Every day I thought up some new argument, but Monsieur Maurice wasn't easily persuaded. Each time I plucked up the nerve to ask, he had the same answer: "You aren't ready yet." He worked quickly even on the hottest days, shoveling nails into his mouth.

"Did you ever swallow one?"

He wouldn't tell me even that. He just laughed, letting a nail drop to the floor.

"There's still plenty of time, Hadara. You need more patience."

"Patience," "balance"—all those entsy-antsy words that grown-ups couldn't do without! I had thought that Monsieur Maurice was different and liked to use short words like "fly" and "takeoff" that he had learned in the circus. Maybe it was the bad influence of Tova, who found some new excuse every day to visit the shoe shop. She had discovered the milky-white slippers and wanted to know whose they were. Monsieur Maurice was annoyed. I had never seen him angry before. He went over to shield the slippers. "You have customers," he said to Tova. "I can see them from here."

"What about the girl? How come you let her stay?"

I hated being called "the girl." I wondered what Tova would say if I called her "Miss Red Nails." I never did find out who gave me the name Hadara. Maybe it was my mother. It was like being named "Citrusella," because *hadar* in Hebrew means "citrus." Sometimes my father put his face next to mine, took a deep breath, and said that I really did smell like a citrus fruit. His nostrils opened like two little doors, and drops of sadness wet his eyes. I was so afraid they would begin to drip that I would quickly think of some joke. Of course I smelled like citrus, I would say: Couldn't he see that I was a real lemon?

Monsieur Maurice Havivel let Tova out the door of his shoe shop. We watched her walk up the street. She didn't turn around to look back. Monsieur Maurice retraced his steps to the shelf with the milky-white slippers—he didn't hide them from me—and said:

"Very well, Hadara. I'll teach you to fly."

four

Monsieur Maurice came from the island of Djerba in North Africa, off the coast of Tunisia. People spoke Arabic and French there, which is why he was called "Monsieur." Islands, I thought, were the perfect place for a circus, because all kinds of strange things happened on them. I had never been on an island myself. I had never even seen a picture of one. I tried imagining what it was like to look out and see water in every direction, but how could I imagine an island when I had hardly ever been to Tel Aviv? Monsieur Maurice said that the Jews who first settled in Djerba were King Solomon's great-grandchildren's great-grandchildren's great-grandchildren, and that everyone still knew from which of Solomon's thousand wives he or she was descended.

"How did your circus get its elephants?" I asked.

"That's easy," said Monsieur Maurice, prying

open the mouth of a brown work boot. "They were left over from the days of Hannibal. Djerba isn't far from Carthage." Without its laces the boot looked like an animal whose teeth had been pulled. I wanted to pet it but was embarrassed. And I had never heard of anyone with the strange name of Hannibal.

In school I tried stretching my legs as much as I could beneath my desk. I could straighten my knees without being noticed and had even learned to curl my little toe into a semicircle. I knew I had to get myself into shape. Every muscle and limb had to be given the message that soon, soon, we were going to fly. Once I was concentrating so hard on my exercises that I didn't even hear the teacher call me up to the board. The whole class burst out laughing, and the teacher asked me to leave and bring a note from my father. I stole a glance at Arele. He wasn't laughing at all.

One day Monsieur Maurice informed me that we were going to start practicing. Perhaps it was because there was talk in the village of a change in the weather. The citrus trees had perked up as if expecting something.

"There's no time to waste," said Monsieur Maurice, sending me off to observe the birds. I recognized the wagtail at once because of its white bib. It looked just like the drawings of it in my nature book. Our teacher explained that every spring the wagtails left for their nesting grounds in Europe and that every autumn they returned. They were, said our teacher with a glance at the open window, our winter friends. Although there was still no sign of real rain, I found a few wagtails by the irrigation pond near the packing house. They had refused to give up and had made up their minds to stay, just like the milky-white slippers on Monsieur Maurice's shelf.

During the day each wagtail went its separate way; but when evening came, they all came home to sleep together in the trees. That was a little like a *kibbutz*, I thought, although of course they had no way of knowing it. Flying was something they did all the time. It made me jealous. A little flap of their wings and they were already in the air, swooping down without warning on the crates of oranges left by the entrance to the packing house and taking off again. Nothing was simpler for them. But then again, maybe it made them jealous to see us open our mouths and talk.

I watched the birds for whole days at a time, especially the wagtails. I knew each one of them and had even given some of them names. They really were well-trained. Even the little babies learned to fly in a hurry. What did the wagtails know that we didn't? Monsieur Maurice didn't have an answer. I swore to keep at it. I would learn by imitating the birds' movements and using my arms like wings until the wind lifted me into the air. I kept a special notebook, in which I wrote down important things, and filled it with drawings of wings. "It takes discipline," said Monsieur Maurice. "You have to practice every day and not give up. That's what the trapeze artists did in our circus." He explained to me that the hardest part was when you had just let go of the bar and were reaching out for the hoop.

"Suppose you miss?" I asked. Monsieur Maurice said that being afraid was part of it.

Despite your fear you reached out with your arms and prayed that your fingers would get a good grip on the hoop. I couldn't imagine Tova from the notions store as a trapeze artist or a wagtail. When she thought no one was looking, she stuffed herself with imported chocolates. No wagtail would ever touch a piece of chocolate. Trapeze artists were light and thin, just like me, and by the time they were perfect at grasping the hoop after millions of hours of practice, they really were able to fly.

"A wardrobe," said Monsieur Maurice, "is no place to practice flying. It may be the highest point in the house, but the ceiling hides the sky. And if you can't see the sky, you can't fly."

f i v e

"What are you jumping up and down for?" asked my father when he came home one evening from the grove. He put on the table some meatballs that Tova had made for us that day, took a bite, and filled my plate with them.

"Are they any good?" I asked suspiciously.

"Tova is an excellent cook," said my father. He must have been feeling pretty hungry to pay her such a compliment. "Are you trying to be the national jumping champion?"

I shrugged. How could I tell him that I wanted to be the one and only national flier? He wouldn't have understood. He would only have said that I was wasting my time and should be reading books instead.

His eyes slowly shut as he ate. "How was school today?" he asked automatically. It was his usual question, and when I started to answer, I saw that he was too tired to listen. Only my mentioning Arele made him sit up suddenly in his chair.

"Zussman's son? Is he a friend of yours?"

He fell asleep right after supper without even taking off his shoes. He lay on the faded sofa by the dining table with his head thrown back, looking like a chopped-down tree. It was a little scary, and I reached out to touch his shoulder and felt better when he moved. I gently untied his shoelaces. He opened his eyes for a second without seeing me and murmured something I couldn't make out. At first I thought it was my mother's name, but I probably imagined it. I took off his big boots, which were covered with dust. One of the heels was ripped, and I put the boots by the door, where I would remember to take them to Monsieur Maurice. Since my father wasn't looking, I took one last jump before going to bed. It didn't wake him. If anyone ever starts a circus in this country, I thought, and not just one more kibbutz after another, I'll be the first to sign up.

I began by jumping from the sand pile in our backyard, but soon I went on to harder jumps, and Monsieur Maurice was satisfied with my progress. Every now and then he stepped out of his shoe shop to see what I was up to. Each time I jumped, I made a mark on the ground where I landed, and the mark kept moving farther. Monsieur Maurice said that even in his circus no one had learned so fast. Next I piled some books on the sand to make it higher. The thickest books I could find in the house were the volumes of the morning newspaper that my father bound each year. To add even more height, I started going to the public library and asking the village's one and only librarian for the biggest books she had. She was thrilled to lend them to me, and I exchanged books three times a week to keep her from suspecting anything. Everything went smoothly until Tova from the notions store told my father why the 1948 volume of *The Morning* had sand in it. He hit the ceiling, because that was the year in which the State of Israel was established. My father rarely raised his voice at me, but now he took the heavy volume, stuck it under his arm, and said I had disappointed him. The year 1948, he said, was "a historic year" and he hadn't missed a single issue in it.

I was only four in 1948 and didn't remember

much except for my mother stroking my hair and saying in a soft voice that we were fighting for our independence and that it would be our last war. By the time I grew up and was a big girl, Israel would be at peace.

The volumes of old newspapers were kept in the tall wardrobe with the summer or winter clothes. I could tell that my father never looked at them by the thick layer of dust on them. Since no one read old newspapers anyway, I had thought I might as well use them to jump from. Besides, I was sure that they would be happy to be out in the sun for a while.

"Never mind," said Monsieur Maurice. "We had problems in our circus too. You always do. It's rather odd to want to fly, and not everyone understands. No one remembers anymore that once Jews flew on Djerba." He glanced at the milky-white slippers and ran a hand across the silver threads. I asked if he thought their owner would ever come for them. I forgot to ask if the elephants from Carthage had wings.

I tried picturing it. I would fly over the whole village. I would look down and see the one and only grocery, the one and only drugstore, the one and only junk cart. The street separating the farmers' houses from the workers' would look like a shoelace from the notions store. And if I felt like it, I would fly even farther, even as far as Tel Aviv. Wouldn't that be something!

Monsieur Maurice wouldn't agree to show me how to do it. It didn't matter how much I begged him. I thought that perhaps he was afraid of being seen and made fun of by Tova, but I wasn't sure that he cared as much about Tova as Tova cared about him. He wouldn't even eat the fancy chocolates she kept giving him. She never offered me any, even though she could see my mouth was watering each time she took one from her apron pocket while she cooked for us. When she stirred the pots, her red nails looked like blood. I didn't like her food and I felt sorry for the man who would marry her. Monsieur Maurice ate only bread and olives, and I began to eat them too, because I was sure that was what made him so light. Anyone living on an island like Djerba had to be ready to take off and fly away at a moment's notice. The wagtails did it every year, except for those who didn't want to leave anymore and stayed on as immigrants.

It was all I could think of. At night I dreamed I was flying, and when I walked in the streets of the village, I kept imagining what I would look like soaring overhead. Everyone would understand at last why I was so thin. I'd make sure to fly low enough for them all to get a good look and shout something up to me. Not that I would answer. Trapeze artists never talked when they were reaching for the hoop. Monsieur Maurice remembered his circus down to the last detail. He remembered what each performer wore, the feathers on the heads of the horses, the way the lion yawned, and how you got the elephants to stand on their hind legs.

"Did you train the animals with whips?" I asked worriedly.

"No one ever threatened anyone in our circus, and no person or animal was ever harmed."

"It must have been a very strange circus," I said.

"Like a dream," said Monsieur Maurice, terribly quietly. I tried figuring out what he meant, but just then Rina Neumann stepped into the shoe shop and our conversation ended.

I wanted to surprise him. I might not have been King Solomon's great-granddaughter's great-granddaughter's great-granddaughter, but I wanted him to know that in Israel too there were Jews who still knew how to fly.

six

Although our village was flat, there was a hill in the middle of the farmers' part that could be seen from everywhere. We were very proud of it and called it Devil Mountain, even if anyone who had seen a real mountain knew it was only a lump of dirt.

Once, years ago, when I was still a baby, someone heard strange voices on the hill at night and woke up the whole village with his shouts. All of the people ran outside in their pajamas, and the one and only village watchman came on the double with his rifle. Searchlights were beamed on the hill and a cat was discovered, caught in a briar patch. It had fought all night to get free, and its wails had sounded like the shrieks of a devil to the man who sounded the alarm. The leaves and branches in its fur made it look like a monster. No one ever found out who it was who'd shouted, despite all the guesses in the village.

My father, from whom I heard the story, was still curious to know. He told me that the only person in the village to stay indoors that night was my mother, who was sure that devils only lived in other countries and that none had come to Israel.

Ever since then, the hill was known as Devil Mountain, and whenever we passed it, we children used to shout, "Devil, begone!" It was a way of being on the safe side, just in case some little devil really had made its home among the bushes in the middle of our village. Rina Neumann didn't like Devil Mountain and made all kinds of detours to avoid it, which wasn't easy, especially since it bordered on Arele Zussman's backyard. Rina said it was a worse place than the cemetery, which lay beyond the citrus groves at the end of the village. And that was a place I never went.

So I chose Devil Mountain for my secret training ground, far from the probing eyes of Tova, who had begun to smell a rat. So had I, because she was coming to cook for us even on days when she wasn't supposed to and kept asking me what my father's favorite food was.

"What can I make him this weekend that will be really special?" she wanted to know. She never asked, "What can I make the two of you?"

Hanukkah vacation was a good time to train. The rains were still only a lazy drizzle, and the farmers were becoming very worried. The drought wasn't affecting just them, either. From my window I could see that Monsieur Maurice's shoe shop had fewer customers than usual. The farmers' children had begun going barefoot, and their parents told them that if it rained, there might be money to fix their shoes next year. Twice a week there were emergency meetings about the citrus trees that went on for hours. Arele's father even came to such a meeting in our house. The drought mattered more to him than his feud, although he couldn't resist saying when he arrived: "So this is where you decided to build that house of yours!"

My father didn't answer.

I knew every corner of the Zussmans' house, which looked tiny from the top of Devil Mountain. I always took along my notebook with the wagtail drawings and a stick to mark my jumps. By now I knew the words I had learned from Monsieur Maurice better than anything I ever studied for school: I would "take to the air." The breeze would "catch" my braid. It would "get to know me" and realize that I was its "friend and not its foe." After all, I only wanted to fly.

Each time I jumped, the stick moved a little farther, which made me sure that I was on the right track. I started counting to ten as soon as my feet left the ground and tried counting higher with every jump. The wind would get to know me—it had better! I was so busy jumping and counting that at first I paid no attention to the strange sounds coming from the bushes. I must be imagining them, I told myself, even giving myself a slap on the back like my father when he wanted to cheer me up.

But the strange sounds continued, coming now from one side and now from another. They made a kind of growly *gr-r-r-r* that was mocking and menacing at once. I froze. My legs wouldn't obey me. I was sure that the hill was inhabited by devils after all. They had been waiting for me in the bushes all this time, special devils that were active even during Hanukkah and in the daytime, too, not just after midnight. Perhaps, the awful thought occurred to me, the dead made sounds like that too.

I turned and ran, leaving my stick behind on the ground. I dropped my wagtail notebook, too. For a second I debated stopping to pick it up, but the frightening growl came again, from the very next bush, and I scooted down the hill as fast as I could.

The wind was whistling in my ears as though it were running too. How could I stupidly have forgotten to shout, "Devil, begone"? Now it was too late. I heard a patter of feet behind me.

"Mama! Here it comes!!!"

I was halfway down the hill when I caught sight of Arele peeking out from behind a bush. He was rolling on the ground with laughter. I could feel my face burn and my fingers curl into fists.

"What are you doing?" I screamed at the top of my voice. "You stutterer you!"

The laughter stopped short. He picked himself up and began to follow the path that led to the backyard of his house. He was all covered with leaves, but he didn't bother brushing them off. Even though he walked quickly, it was with a stoop. I began running after him.

"Arele, wait!"

I wanted to tell him that I hadn't meant it, but the words were stuck in my throat.

seven

A sudden hush came over Devil Mountain. I could hear the leaves rustling slightly and the gaily skipping birds pecking for worms. I was glad that they couldn't understand anything.

Arele didn't always stutter. It happened only when he was excited and couldn't get the words out, and they tumbled out broken and crushed. When he was called to the board, the teachers waited patiently. The first two words always gave him a hard time, but afterward they flowed more easily. Rina Neumann would look at him with her big eyes and send him encouraging smiles, and even the boys who snickered behind his back didn't dare do so to his face. Arele was not only the best swimmer around, he was the strongest boy his age.

My training had hit a snag. I could never come back to Devil Mountain, not even if Monsieur Maurice insisted that it was the best place. If you asked me, there was a curse on it even if there were no devils. Or rather, there was a different kind of devil, the kind that could come bursting out of you without warning. If Monsieur Maurice had known how I had hurt Arele's feelings, he would have been very angry. Once, he told me, a bear tamer had come to his circus with some wonderfully acrobatic bears who brought down the house and sold out every performance. After a while, though, the other performers discovered that the man treated the bears cruelly, and even though they could stand up and dance a waltz, he was asked to leave the circus. Long ago, the circus performers told him, people and animals had shared Noah's Ark, and ever since then they were equal in God's eyes.

"No animal is inferior to a human being, not even a clumsy black bear," said Monsieur Maurice.

"Don't human beings sometimes think that even other human beings are inferior?" I asked.

Usually, Monsieur Maurice liked answering my questions, but there were some he never replied to, no matter how long I waited. I never knew which questions would be which. Some, like this one, made his face change, and then he turned away as if to hide something or else pretended to be very busy. If he happened to be polishing a pair of shoes when this happened, they would come out as shiny as fresh oranges.

I knew the answer even without him, though. Some people really did think that other people were inferior. Don't ask me how I knew it—I just did.

When I saw that Monsieur Maurice wasn't answering, I asked something else: "Were there any birds in your circus?"

"Birds can't be trained. There's no cage that will hold them."

The wagtail notebook lay beside me. All its wings had gotten dirty. On its back I suddenly noticed a strange drawing that Monsieur Maurice must have made, although I don't know when he did it. Above it he had written "Cage" in nice, round letters, like those you make when you've just learned to write, but what he had drawn was a long, high barbed-wire fence with searchlights shining down on it. I had never seen such a cage before. I couldn't imagine what kind of animal it was for. Maybe, I thought, it was for man-eating beasts, or maybe Monsieur Maurice simply didn't know how to draw. Not everyone who could fix shoes and fly was also an artist. Not even a circus performer could do everything.

I laid the wagtail notebook in my lap and reflected that Monsieur Maurice had never told me just what he did in the circus. Had he been a sword swallower? A fire eater? A tiger tamer? A bareback rider? Neither did I know how all those big animals had gotten to Djerba.

I kept thinking about all of this as I walked down the hill in order to put off reaching the bottom of the path. The devil inside me had crawled back into a shell as thick as a grapefruit peel. The path led straight to Arele's backyard, which I didn't want to go near. Arele's father hadn't talked to my father because my father had moved to a different part of the village, which was an odd reason not to talk to someone. And now Arele wouldn't talk to me because I had called him a stutterer, which was a very good reason indeed.

My legs refused to leave the path. As though they had a will of their own, they walked right into Arele Zussman's backyard instead of taking me home.

eight

The door of the shack was open, but I didn't see anyone. The Zussmans' laundry was flapping on the line. It looked dry to me, and I thought that Arele's mother ought to take it in, just in case the rain surprised us after all.

"Arele!" I called.

My feet made up their own mind again and advanced to the door of the shack.

"Go away!"

I heard him over the flapping of the wash. I noticed that his gym shorts were hanging out to dry, too, and for some reason I blushed.

It was dark in the shack, and for a second I felt blindfolded. In one corner I made out a pale silhouette. I knew that it was Arele sitting and hugging his knees. I stood in the doorway, not knowing whether to step inside.

"Why waste your time on stutterers?"

The last two words couldn't get past the lump in his throat. He coughed for a while to hide his stutter and then spat them out.

"I thought . . . I thought . . ." I stuttered a little on purpose myself. "I thought that you were the devil of Devil Mountain."

"What do you go up there every day for? Don't you have anything better to do with your vacation? I'm sure your father could use some help in his grove. When I'm in school, my mother helps my father."

Arele rose from his corner. My eyes had gotten used to the dark. The shack was full of books. Pictures of oranges and grapefruits were plastered on the walls, and some citrus branches lay on a table.

"What are those?"

"It's none of your business!" He snatched them from the table.

"Soon I'll be seeing all this from above."

"What is that supposed to mean?"

He put a branch back on the table, and I touched it.

"The citrus trees don't lose their leaves even in winter. No matter when I'm up there, I'll look down and they'll be green."

"That's called an evergreen," said Arele

knowledgeably, his stutter not so bad anymore. "I know all about citrus trees. Next year I'm going to agricultural school."

He opened the windows of the shack to let the light in. Now I could see that it was full of green plants.

"So you've been climbing Devil Mountain to plant trees?" asked Arele. "It's not the right soil for a citrus grove."

"How do you know? When our grandparents founded this village, they didn't believe you could plant citrus trees in sand either, and look what there is now."

Arele pointed out that in those days my grandfather and Arele's grandfather had lived with the other farmers. I wasn't interested in talking about old feuds, and so I changed the subject.

"Do you think citrus trees would grow on an island?"

Arele wanted to know why I was suddenly so interested in islands.

"Because of Monsieur Maurice Havivel," I said. "He comes from the island of Djerba."

The only island Arele had ever heard of was

Cyprus. He said it wasn't far from us, across the water from Haifa. Arele claimed that his father had once taken a boat there and brought back baby lemon trees but I found that hard to believe.

"I'm grafting new strains of citrus in this shack," he said with open pride. "But you wouldn't know about such things. Ever since your father moved—"

"Our groves are kept as well as anyone's," I said angrily. "And I do too help my father sometimes. I may not know much about grafts and things, but every summer I lime the tree trunks against pests, and I can also dig irrigation holes. And I can climb to the top of the tallest tree and find fruit that everyone missed."

I wanted to go home, but Arele picked up a branch and held it to the light.

"My father says that we citrus growers should live together."

"Not everything has to be done according to the rules."

"Like what?"

"Like flying!"

nine

The light was soft in the window of the shack, not like the burning yellow light of summer. The branch shook in Arele's hand. I wasn't sure what he was trying to do with it.

"Look, Hadara. Take a look at this leaf in the light."

I held it up so close that it touched my nose. It had a good smell. There were lots of transparent little spots all over it. Although I must have seen millions of citrus leaves in my life, I had never paid attention before to what was hidden in their greenness. A plain little leaf had as much in it as our tall wardrobe with all its clothes.

"I know all this leaf's secrets," said Arele. "I'm going to invent new strains of trees."

He stood in the middle of the shack like our village's one and only mayor giving his New Year's speech to us schoolchildren and explained to me what went into starting a new grove.

First, you had to raise baby trees in a nursery from sweet and sour lemon seeds. Next, you moved them to the field where you were going to plant your grove. Then you cultivated the ground with a deep plowing. . . . Although I already knew most of it, I was fascinated, because Arele Zussman didn't stutter even once. The words flowed from his mouth like freshly squeezed juice. He was a born citrus grower—not like me, who wanted to fly or join a circus.

Arele was so carried away by his own speech that he decided to show me how to graft a tree. He picked up a baby tree trunk that he called the "stock" and a small branch with a bud that he called the "scion."

"They're like a father and a mother. The orange will be their child. You'll have to wait seven years before you can taste it, though."

I was thinking of how different Arele's trees would look from above. As I flew overhead, he would wave to me and shout up his latest invention. Orangines, tangemons, grapequats, lemonges: I could think up the names myself.

"Did you know, Arele, that the fruit that

Adam and Eve ate in the Garden of Eden may not have been an apple?"

He raised his eyebrows. "How do you know?" I thought I detected a slight stutter again, but I couldn't be sure.

"It doesn't say in the Bible that it was an apple. It just says it was a fruit. For all we know, it could have been a grapefruit."

Arele laughed and said that the serpent could never have tempted Eve with anything so bitter.

I took my wagtail notebook and said I had to go.

"Will you come back to Devil Mountain?"

"I don't know."

He shut the windows and walked me outside.

"I'll let you know if the graft takes. And if it doesn't, I'll try again. Before the vacation is over, I'll invent a new strain."

We crossed his backyard. I noticed that someone, no doubt his mother, had taken in the wash. Tova sometimes offered to do the same for us, but I wouldn't let her. She was always looking at my clothes to see if they didn't have some loose stitch or torn hem. As it was, she made too many comments about how "You can see that this house needs a woman."

All that was left on the Zussmans' laundry line were the brightly colored clothespins. Even Devil Mountain suddenly looked awfully small. How could I have imagined that there was actually a devil in one of its bushes?

Arele walked me to the street that divided the citrus growers' homes from the workers'. In the distance we could see the Hanukkah menorah on top of the town hall, which was the most important building in the village. Three of its eight candles were already lit.

"I'd better hurry," I said. "My father quits work early so that we can light the candles and sing Hanukkah songs together." I continued walking, but Arele had stopped.

"You know," he said, and I could hear him clearly even though we were now standing on opposite sides of the street, "when I scared you up there on Devil Mountain, you suddenly screamed for your mother. I would have thought it would have been for your father."

I ran the rest of the way home.

t e n

What flew at night?

I lay in bed, my head beneath the blanket to shut out the world and not to have to see the black ceiling. All the lovely birds were asleep now, resting on the branches with folded wings. Night was rest time for a wing. So what flew at night?

I listened to my father's footsteps on the porch. He too couldn't sleep and was pacing up and down. I could tell exactly where he was because of the loose floor tile at one end of the porch that creaked whenever he stepped on it. His footsteps were heavy. Maybe he also wanted to fly and wasn't telling me. If he could fly, he would pat the heads of the orange trees and tell them not to worry, because the rain would come.

The clothes wardrobe was invisible, swallowed up by the wall. I sat up in bed to make sure that my room was still my room, even in the darkness. The reason birds flew so far was that they weren't happy where they were. They put their babies on their backs and set out. I wasn't happy either, but I had no wings.

My father let out a sigh and said something. Sometimes, when no one was listening, he talked to himself. I would have liked to be a baby bird who climbed on his back and flew off to some place where you didn't have to pray for rain. Not at night, though. At night you couldn't see where you were going. What flew at night?

I got out of bed. A dim light, perhaps the last flicker of the Hanukkah candles, came from the kitchen. The wardrobe threw a large shadow that was darker than the darkness around it, which was darker than the darkness around *it*. I couldn't find my slippers and walked barefoot, groping my way along the walls. Perhaps the night was the giant wing of a huge, sleeping bird that was covering us. There was nothing frightening or dangerous about it: It was just a feathery quilt spread over me and my father and Monsieur Maurice and the whole village. And over Arele Zussman.

I had come home that night to a platter of Hanukkah pancakes and a bowl of Hanukkah doughnuts, both made by Tova. My father thanked her and ate heartily, and Tova was in seventh heaven. She even stayed to light the candles with us. My father wanted to invite Monsieur Maurice, too, but Tova made a face.

"Why not let it be just the three of us?" she said in a sugary voice. She thought it would make up for having yelled at me for coming home late.

My father said that Monsieur Maurice was all alone and that this was his first Hanukkah in Israel. And so he was invited and listened in silence to the blessings and the songs. Tova said my father sang wonderfully and told him he could do a better job leading services than our village's one and only cantor, although if you ask me, he was off-key. Monsieur Maurice did not seem impressed by his voice either, because he did not compliment him on it at all. Tova's nail polish was a flaming red. I was sure she had freshened it up for the evening and hoped she hadn't done it while frying the pancakes or kneading the batter for the doughnuts. If I ever stopped biting my nails, I would color them green and let them grow like leaves.

❖   ❖   ❖

My father's footsteps halted on the porch. I couldn't hear him anymore.

So what flew at night?

Moths flew at night. Bats flew at night. Ghosts flew at night. No, there was no such thing as ghosts. The dead stayed under the ground in their stone cages. Even if I dug the deepest trench for them, they couldn't come out.

I went out to the porch. My father was sitting in the rocking chair that had once been my grandfather's, smoking a cigarette. He inhaled deeply and blew smoke rings into our dark garden. He smoked only when he was very worried about something.

"You're not sleeping?"

"I just woke up. I heard a noise."

He made room for me in the rocking chair.

"This drought will be the end of us," he said.

"What's going to happen?"

He inhaled again. "The groves will dry up."

"Will we have to go back to living in our old house?"

"No," he said. "This is the only house we have now."

It wasn't much of a house. It was small and had cracks in the plaster and leaky pipes. The floor tiles were crooked, too, but I didn't care. I liked everything just the way it was.

"You need a new pair of shoes," my father said. "And a new dress. But the damn rain has forgotten us."

We rocked together. Even though it was an old chair that came from our old house, it didn't creak at all.

I had once seen a grove that dried up. It was on a school outing. There still was lime on the tree trunks, but the irrigation holes had filled up with earth. The irrigation ditches were full of dry leaves, branches, and rotted fruit. All kinds of pests had bored big holes in the trees, which no longer had any leaves. I thought it looked like a graveyard and kept my eyes shut till we were out of it.

"Where have you been?" Tova had screamed at me when I came running from Devil Mountain. She was standing in the kitchen doorway as though she owned it. "Your father will ask me about you tonight, and what am I supposed to tell him? That you disappear for hours on end or else spend your time shining shoes? You're wild. You have no self-control. Into the house with you!"

I gripped my wagtail notebook as tightly as I could, my fingers feeling like the cage that Monsieur Maurice had drawn.

"Don't you tell me what to do! You're not my mother!"

That had been hours ago. Afterward, we lit the Hanukkah candles, and now the last of them had gone out. My father put out his cigarette and stood behind the chair, rocking me. I shut my eyes and thought that it was a little like flying. If I could fly, I would tie all the clouds to a string and pull them back down with me.

eleven

"I can't wait any longer!" I exclaimed. "You have to understand, Monsieur Maurice."

His mouth was full of nails again. He was fixing four pairs of shoes at once. I tapped my foot beneath the table while waiting for him to finish.

"Monsieur Maurice, the groves are drying up. Something has to be done."

He slipped his hand into a large boot and looked it over carefully.

"Leave that to your father."

"My father is desperate too."

"Desperate?" Monsieur Maurice threw me a look as sharp as a nail. "You don't know what desperate means."

I picked up a shoe and stuck my hand into it, bitten fingernails and all.

"It's really urgent, Monsieur Maurice." My hand vanished into the shoe.

"You're not ready yet." He gently removed the shoe from my hand.

My fingernails were out in the open again, but this time I didn't try hiding them.

Among the Jews settling on the island of Djerba, Monsieur Maurice told me, were priests who had served in the Temple in Jerusalem. They had brought with them a most precious object, which they carefully guarded all the way like a great treasure. "Can you imagine what it was like to carry a door from the Temple all that distance on your back?"

"A door from the Temple?"

Monsieur Maurice nodded. "Yes, indeed," he said. "They took it when the Temple was destroyed. They were determined to bring it, despite all the difficulties on the way. They were sure that they and the door would reach Djerba safely. They never gave up."

"Did you ever see the door?"

Monsieur Maurice smiled, which was something he didn't do often. It was like a window being opened in his face. Of course he had seen it. Every child on Djerba knew it was kept in the El-Ghariba Synagogue.

"El-Ghariba?" I repeated the word like a magic spell. "What does that mean?" I tried imitating the way Monsieur Maurice pronounced the first letter of "Ghariba," with an "R" that burbled up from deep in his throat. There was no such sound in Hebrew.

" 'El-Ghariba' means 'The Wondrous One' in Arabic." His face beamed. Then the light went out of his eyes, and he said, "But some people say it means 'The Forlorn One.' "

A synagogue that is like a person—how strange, I thought. But I didn't say so to Monsieur Maurice. In my mind I kept trying to make that deep, throaty Arabic "R."

"Do you miss Djerba?"

His smile disappeared slowly, like a sky that takes all day to cloud over.

"It's my home."

"But how can it be? Israel is your home now."

Monsieur Maurice put a boot on his other hand.

"You're right. It can't be. But it is."

"How can someone have two homes?"

He looked at the boots on his hands. "How can someone have two shoes?"

"One for the right foot and one for the left. You yourself told me that they can't be separated."

Monsieur Maurice arranged a long row of nails, all the same length, on the table in front of him.

"That's just it," he said. "You can't separate two homes either."

When he saw that I didn't get it, he explained that a person's two feet were not identical. Pairs were not the same as twins. One foot could be shorter, or thicker, or rounder than the other. And the two sides of a face were different, too. I wanted to run to the mirror and see if it was true, but there was no mirror in Monsieur Maurice's shop.

"One shoe can be too tight and not the other," he said, adding more nails to the row, which had almost reached the end of the table.

I asked him which shoe was the tight one: Israel or Djerba? The row of nails now spanned the whole table. He answered that a person comes to Israel barefoot. You don't need shoes at all.

"That's right," I said. "You need wings." That's when I decided that I was going to go ahead and take the plunge.

Suddenly I noticed that something was missing from the top shelf. The milky-white slippers were gone.

"She's back!" I cried excitedly. But Monsieur Maurice didn't hear me. He was no longer in his shop. I stepped outside and saw him being handed a shoe by someone from the next village. That's how famous he was. It was a single shoe, with a huge hole in the heel.

I looked at it and remembered Monsieur Maurice telling me that he had once seen a huge mountain of children's shoes. I didn't ask him when and where that was. My instinct told me not to, because he wouldn't have answered.

The man from the next village needed his shoe in a hurry, and Monsieur Maurice agreed to fix it on the spot and invited its owner in for a cup of Turkish coffee while he waited. I didn't ask about the slippers again. I just sat there watching the hole in the heel disappear. Monsieur Maurice put on a new sole, trimmed the edges, cleaned the shoe well, and made it look almost new. Before returning it, he polished and brushed it several times. The customer from the next village reached out to take it, but Monsieur Maurice insisted on one last buffing, after which he took a little brush and touched up the corners in places you couldn't even see. By now the man was impatiently on his feet.

"Are you good at drawing, Monsieur Maurice?" I asked when the customer was gone.

He shook his head, still holding the little brush.

I felt relieved. The picture on the back of my wagtail notebook was just a badly drawn cage, then. It wasn't some kind of mistake. Monsieur Maurice simply couldn't draw.

t w e l v e

The night before, I was a nervous wreck. I couldn't make up my mind what to wear. At last the whole village was going to see me fly.

I took all my clothes from the wardrobe and spread them out on my bed. There weren't that many of them, but I didn't need more. I returned my only dress to the wardrobe at once: I would have to be crazy to fly over the village in a dress. My elastic gym shorts would be fine, but they might get a little chilly so high up. In the end, though, I decided that they were the best fly wear I had. It was too bad I didn't have a trapeze costume. Maybe once everyone saw what I could do, the village's one and only seamstress would make me a special outfit.

I laid my two best blouses on the bed. One was green and one was yellow. The green one was out of the question, because I didn't want to be mistaken for a big leaf torn loose from a tree. The yellow one wasn't much better, since

Arele Zussman might think I was a flying lemon. I kept looking back and forth between them and finally settled for the yellow one.

It was just my luck that my father came home early that evening. The emergency drought meetings had stopped. There was nothing more to talk about. There was nothing to do but wait.

"Are you rearranging your clothes?" he asked, picking up the yellow blouse. I took that as a sign that I should wear it.

"It's missing a button," he said, sending me off to Tova's notions shop. Carrying the blouse, I ran all the way up the street, only to find her turning out the lights and closing for the day. "I wouldn't open up again for anyone but you," she said. "I hope you appreciate it."

"Thanks a million, Tova," I said humbly, waiting for her to turn around before I stuck out my tongue at her. I always did things like that behind her back. It may have been rude, but it was good for me.

She took out all her button boxes and began going through them.

"Where are the yellows?" she mumbled to

herself, rummaging in a box. I waited patiently.

"Here, you look too," Tova ordered me. I began taking the covers off box after box, searching for the right yellow button. Now and then Tova bent down to a bottom drawer as if she were searching there, too; but when she straightened up, she had something in her mouth, and I knew she was eating chocolates. The more quietly she tried sucking on them, the more her mouth puckered at the corners. I couldn't help smiling. Because of me, the poor thing couldn't enjoy her chocolates. And she had to bend down again every time she wanted to swallow.

"Does your father like chocolate?"

"I don't know."

"And your mother? Did she?"

I didn't answer.

"I get a box of chocolate bonbons every week from my aunt, who lives abroad. If your father likes them, I'll be happy to bring him some."

Luckily, I found a yellow button just then, and that was the end of that.

Just you wait, Miss Tova Notions, just you wait until you see me tomorrow: You'll come

running to give me a whole box of chocolates—
me, not my father! And you'll want everyone to
know that a yellow button on my blouse comes
from your notions store, because I'll not only
be the one and only flier in our village, I'll be
the one and only flier in the whole state of
Israel!

Tova threaded a needle with a yellow thread
and began to sew. I told her she didn't have to
because I could do it myself, but she said my
father would expect it of her and that she had to
"be a mother" to me. It was all I could do to
keep from slapping her. I tried keeping my mind
on tomorrow.

"Yellow isn't your color," said Tova, breaking
off the thread between her teeth. "It makes you
look like an old broom. Why don't you wear
red?" She glanced at her nails. The polish was all
peeling, but it didn't seem to bother her. She
thought she had the most beautiful hands in the
world.

"A woman has to take good care of her
hands," she announced expertly with a look at
my bitten nails—because of which, she said, no
one would ever want to marry me. I took a deep

breath and wondered how much more I would have to go through for one button.

Tova went on and on. She talked about my mother and she talked about my father, but by now I wasn't listening. I had dived deep into myself, where I was going over Monsieur Maurice's last and most important flying lesson.

Monsieur Maurice had told me that I mustn't think too much before I jumped. He had said that I should lift my head as high as I could, find some point in the sky, and aim right at it.

"How can I find a point in the sky?" I asked. "The sky is all the same."

"That's what you think. The higher you get, the more you'll discover things you never dreamed of. You'll see that the sky isn't even blue."

Tova folded my yellow blouse and turned off the lights in her store. The blouse shone in the dark. It took her a long time to slip the key into the lock. All at once she sighed. It was really more like a sob. "I wish I had a husband," she said. For a second, though not for more than that, I felt sorry for her.

thirteen

For seven years the tree had grown while every-one waited. It had been looked after, worried over, watered, pruned, and connected to a special irrigation hole. The tree's mother and father—their names were Stock and Scion, or perhaps it was the other way around—never left it alone for a minute. And now I was climbing to the top of it, all the way to the highest branch.

I had chosen the tallest tree in our citrus grove. My father had gone that morning to the port in Jaffa to pick up a shipment of Valencia saplings from Spain. He said that the drought would make the Valencias tougher competition than usual, but I wasn't worried. The oranges we grew had thick skins and were called Shamoutis, while the Spanish Valencias had thin skins. Our Shamoutis had a special taste all their own and came apart into sections as easily as the petals of a flower.

My tree—that's already how I thought of it—was waiting for me as if it knew what I was going to do. In order to get halfway up the trunk, from which the lower branches had been pruned, I had to take the picker's ladder from the packing house. A few dead leaves from the tangerine harvest were still on its rungs. It was the time of afternoon when people rose from their naps for a glass of tea or milk. As soon as they stepped outside, they would see me overhead. It would be the end of the drought, too.

A couple of birds took off in fright from the tree. They weren't wagtails, just plain birds that didn't understand why I was invading their home. Getting to the top of the ladder was easy. Then I clung to a branch and slowly nudged the ladder over with my foot to the next tree so that I could have my own tree to myself. I didn't feel the scratches from the branches. I didn't even bother to try spotting our house or Monsieur Maurice's shop, or Devil Mountain and the Zussmans' house. I looked for Monsieur Maurice's point—that magical place in the sky that you had to find before you could fly.

The higher I got, the more green fruits there were on the branches. Soon they would be ready to pick. One, which was orange and wrinkled-looking, must have been left over from the year before. How did my father know when one season was over and a new one had begun? If I spent my whole life among orange trees like he did, I suppose I'd know that secret too.

I didn't look down, because Monsieur Maurice had said that you had to look and think up when you climbed. The ground, he said, was like a weight dragging you down, and you mustn't let your eyes get trapped on it. The leaves stroked my skin like soft hands without nails. I thought how each was full of lacy little circles like the ones Arele had showed me.

I stretched my legs and spread my arms, feeling my bitten fingernails grow longer. I was touching the sky—or maybe the sky was touching me. It still looked blue, but slightly faded. Monsieur Maurice was right. High up, the blue disappeared. I felt as if someone or something was gripping me by the roots of my hair. My face strained upward. That was the only direction there was. There was no more down anymore, no more earth, and no one buried beneath it.

I shut my eyes.

I thought of the wagtails with their white bibs.

I thought of how *up* was the only way a tree grew.

And of how the nicest things were over our heads. Now I was going to reach them.

I can fly! *I can fly!!!*

The earth was hard and dry. I had never realized before how cruel it could be, how there was nothing it wouldn't steal from me. When a tree cried, no one heard it. Sometimes no one heard a person cry either. Trees don't shed any tears upon the cruel earth, but people do. For what the earth has taken from them. It is hard. It had beaten me and hurt me, but I wasn't going to cry.

The sky was yellow and then gray. All the blue was gone from it, but I kept my eyes shut and on my point. It was mine alone. No one else could see it, not even Monsieur Maurice. He had a point of his own.

Although I lay on the ground, my head was in the sky. I didn't feel the terrible pain. King Solomon's great-grandchildren's great-grandchildren's great-grandchildren must have been wonders to find a faraway island like Djerba. I bet that even he, the wisest of men, had never heard of it.

fourteen

The sky drifted off and left me all alone. The trees stirred above me. A leaf came twirling down, which was very odd, because orange trees were evergreens. They never lost their leaves and stood trembling in the cold. It was I who was cold now. From where I lay, my tree was no longer the tallest in the grove. It was just another tree. I looked for my point in the receding sky, but it was hidden by the leaves. The little oranges shook in the breeze. Or was it I who was shaking, as if I were still flying?

I had lost my point. It was gone. So were my wings. I wasn't light enough. I sank into the hard earth. It pulled me down and dug me into it. I wanted to scream, but the words were gone too.

"Hadara! Hadara!"

I hadn't known that trees could talk. Or maybe it was the wagtails that were calling me.

If King Solomon could speak the language of the plants and animals, maybe I could too, now that I had flown a little.

"Hadara! Hadara! Hadara!"

I opened my eyes. Arele Zussman was kneeling beside me. He wasn't a wagtail or a tree. He was just Arele from my class in school.

"What happened?"

I didn't want to tell him.

He bent and touched my leg. It had no feeling.

"We have to get you home," said Arele. He fingered my leg carefully, as if it were a branch felled by a storm. "Come on."

I tried dragging myself, but I was bound to the earth by an invisible rope.

"I can't."

"I'll help you," Arele said. He put his arm around my shoulder and began to pull me slowly along.

"Leave me here."

"Are you crazy? I'm not leaving you anywhere. Don't worry. I'm strong. I can lift you." He didn't stutter even once.

We began to walk. Or rather, he walked and

pulled me along with him. I couldn't put any weight on my leg. It didn't feel connected to my body. Arele kept whispering encouragement and we gradually made progress.

"I was out looking at the trees," he said, "and suddenly I thought I saw someone flying through the air. I must have imagined it."

I bit my lip. I didn't want him to laugh at me. He was the strongest boy in our village, and I was sure that pain was nothing to him. Monsieur Maurice's flying trapeze artists never flew without a net, and here I had gone and crashed on my first flight! Because I wasn't a trapeze artist. I was just a girl in a small village far from Tel Aviv.

Arele began telling me stories. He was trying to make me forget my leg, and so he told me about the citron that came from the southern slopes of the Himalayas, which were the world's highest mountains. They were real mountains, not like the one in our village.

"When did the citron come to Israel?" I asked to help pass the time.

Arele really knew a lot, such as that citrons came to Israel in biblical times, and oranges in the sixteenth century, nearly four hundred years ago.

"They're not such new immigrants, then," I joked, trying to smile.

We were halfway there. Arele said that his father's grove was slightly bigger than my father's but that it didn't matter. And that he never understood why his father was mad at mine, because what difference did it make where you lived? We all lived in the same village.

"How come you know so much about trees?"

"They're more interesting than people," said Arele. His stutter was back again.

We reached the end of the groves and could see the houses of my neighborhood in the distance. In my head I saw a circus tent soaring through the air, and airborne elephants whose big ears were flapping, and lions roaring in the wind with their manes rippling like the sea, and flying Jews. Lots of Monsieur Maurices landing on an island after a long flight. Arele was wrong. People were more interesting than trees. I didn't tell him that, though.

"What's my father going to say?" I asked ruefully.

"You should be glad you didn't break both legs," Arele said.

"You sound just like him."

"Or like your mother," said Arele. He said nothing for a minute and then asked, "Do you remember her?"

The pain was so bad that I couldn't stand up anymore. "I can't go on," I said quietly, but Arele gripped me more strongly and said, "Hang on, we're almost there!"

And then, all at once, it started to rain. It was like a door that had suddenly opened after being knocked on for a long time. Every drop was a little ball of water. Arele began to shout for joy, but excited as he was, he never let go of my shoulder. The rain ran down his face, and you might have thought he was crying if it hadn't been for the big grin that spread up his cheeks all the way to his forehead.

"The trees are saved!" he shouted. "They'll drink up and we'll have water for the year. We'll beat those Valencias yet!"

The villagers came running from their houses. The Turkish barber still had his scissors in his hand. The seamstress opened her window and waved a piece of fabric streaming with white threads. The grocer stepped into the street with a crate of tomatoes, and only Tova stayed inside with her imported chocolates. No one paid Arele and me any attention.

"The drought is over!"

I wondered what they would have shouted if they had seen me flying through the sky.

The earth had turned to mud, clumps of which stuck to our shoes. Monsieur Maurice would have lots of business now, I thought. The leg I dragged behind me left a trail of mud on the sidewalk. My braid was soaking wet and dripped water down my back. Arele tried walking faster. It was pouring buckets now, and a river ran in the street. My pain bobbed up and down on it, and my leg felt like a waterlogged leaf. I was a flop. I couldn't fly. Monsieur Maurice had tried to teach me, but something had gone wrong. If only I knew what.

"How did you find me in the grove?" I asked. We were standing in front of the one and only village clinic. Arele gently took his hand from my shoulder and helped me lean against the door.

"I heard you crying."

He knocked. It took a while for someone to open. The rain beat out a dance rhythm. The drops were so big that they ricocheted from the ground. I wiped my wet cheek. It was a tempest, and it didn't stop for the next three days.

"I never cry," I said. But Arele didn't hear me. He had already joined the celebration in the street.

fifteen

The one and only nurse in our village tried calling the one and only doctor, but he had left early that morning to deliver a baby and had not yet returned. The nurse was not sure how to make a cast, and so she opened a large manual and sent her little son to buy ingredients. I lay on a bed without a peep and thought that getting used to pain was part of my training. Each time I moved, I felt the pain stab me like a pesky wagtail. I stared at the white ceiling and found a point there too. It faded in and out, but each time, I found it again.

The one and only nurse in our village stirred some white plaster in a pot. A few strands of hair escaped from beneath her white nurse's cap and got into the goo. Raindrops ran down the windows. The nurse stirred and sighed, "Now the whole village will turn to mud. There'll be a rash of broken legs and no end of work for me."

Her small son pulled her dress and whispered something in her ear. She gave me a strange look and said, "You fell from a tree? What an odd girl you are. What were you doing up there, reaching for the clouds? That's what happens when children run wild." She made me sound like some kind of criminal.

"I live with my father and we get along fine," I said.

"A father isn't enough," said the nurse, letting her son stir the plaster a little. "Running wild in the streets!"

The little boy splashed plaster with the wooden spoon, and she shouted at him that it wasn't a game. "All he does is get in my hair," grumbled the one and only nurse in our village, testing the white goo with her finger.

Just when I had decided that she looked like the Witch of Endor in the Bible, the door opened and in came Monsieur Maurice.

"What brings you here?" the nurse turned on him. "I suppose you climbed a tree and broke a leg too!"

Monsieur Maurice didn't answer. He put his hand on my leg, which looked as thin as a pruned branch, although you couldn't tell it was broken just from looking at it.

The nurse stared at him, the wooden spoon in her hand dripping plaster. "Just what do you think you're doing, taking measurements for shoes? You won't find any customers here. Can't you see she won't walk again for a while?"

I thought of the mountain of children's shoes that Monsieur Maurice had once seen and broke into a shiver. As if gathering it up, Monsieur Maurice circled my leg with his hand. "This is a very brave leg," he said.

"It's a flop." I turned my head to the wall.

The nurse's little boy said that he wanted a cast on his leg too. The nurse told him I had been irresponsible. "I want one too! I want one too!" he began to cry. She took him aside and said in a whisper, although I heard every word: "She may never walk again." That made him stop crying. He went and stood in a corner, from which he looked at me curiously.

The nurse told Monsieur Maurice that he was in the way and asked him to please go back to his shop and make sure not to slip in the mud, because she didn't have any plaster for more casts.

Monsieur Maurice ignored her and kept his dark eyes on me. Suddenly he reached out and seized the wooden spoon from the pot of plaster. The nurse made no attempt to stop him. She just took up a blocking position in front of the pot. Her nurse's cap was awry.

"I saw the point," I said.

Monsieur Maurice nodded. He put the spoon back in the pot, where it sank quickly into the plaster. I wanted to tell him that I wasn't giving up and would try again, but his eyes warned me not to. Their dark pupils looked like two Djerbas in a wet, white sea.

"The pain is part of my training, isn't it, Monsieur Maurice?"

"You should have waited."

I could feel the anger rise inside me. A flying teacher should have known that his student couldn't wait forever until the whole world was one big drought. What kind of teacher was Monsieur Maurice Havivel? Maybe he no longer remembered anything and was embarrassed to tell me. The nurse announced that the plaster was done. Monsieur Maurice straightened up.

"You weren't ready," he said in a stubborn voice.

"Ready for what?"

I didn't know I had been shouting until I saw the nurse cover her ears. Monsieur Maurice gently released my leg and bent down to lift a shoe from the floor.

"You weren't scared enough to fly for real," he said, hugging my shoe. He sounded different, though I only realized why when he had left. There were no nails in his mouth.

sixteen

My father wasn't furious. Although I was expecting a bad punishment, I didn't get so much as a scolding. He had been on his way to the grove with the baby Valencia trees when he heard what had happened and went straight to the clinic. I wanted to ask him what the thin-skinned Spanish oranges tasted like but decided it wasn't the time for it. Instead of watching me fly through the air, the village watched him carry me like a baby. The cast came up past my knee, and my father held an umbrella over it to keep it from getting soggy in the downpour.

Arele Zussman was waiting by our house. He was still in the same wet clothes and hadn't even put on a raincoat. He opened the door for us.

"You see, Hadara, all you did was break a leg. What luck!"

My father thanked him and said that if any-one needed proof that he was really the strongest boy in the village, this was it. As light as I was, it couldn't have been easy to drag me all the way to the clinic. Arele was shaking with cold, and my father told him to go home before he got sick and ended up in the clinic himself.

"Never mind. As long as it's rained. Why . . . what took it so long?"

"Nobody went to look for it."

I wanted to say that I went, but I didn't. I couldn't bend my leg. From now on I would have to keep it stiff and straight. It would hibernate through the winter.

Father was surprised to see that Monsieur Maurice's shop looked closed. He must be off celebrating with everyone else, he said, even though he wasn't a citrus grower. Five minutes after we got home, Tova arrived. She didn't even knock. She blew in like a storm, wringing her hands and exclaiming, "Oh, my!"

"It's not so terrible," said my father. "A broken leg is only a broken leg."

"She might have broken her head," Tova wailed. "I knew she was up to something. It's all my fault for not keeping an eye on her."

My father tensed. He opened the door for

Tova to leave, but far from getting the hint, she stayed and offered to help. She would do everything, from cleaning the house to nursing me "like a mother." She smiled at me from ear to ear. I didn't smile back.

At first politely and then more firmly, my father said there was no need.

"I hope," said Tova triumphantly, "that she's learned a lesson and jumped from her last tree." With a sigh she added, "She should only end up with nothing worse than a limp."

My father hugged me and told Tova in plain words to go home, because the two of us wanted to be alone. If she was hurt, she didn't show it. She even announced on her way out that she would drop by again in the morning before opening her store.

My father never asked what I had been doing in a treetop. Although I suspected he knew the truth, he didn't say a word.

I took off my yellow blouse, which by now looked more like a dishrag than my best shirt, hung it on the back of a chair, and thought of the scare I must have given the wagtails. They must have thought the sun was falling down. For a second I really had flown. I could remember it exactly—free of the earth, with the air all around me—but it had lasted only a second.

"Close your eyes," said my father.

He popped some sweet orange sections into my mouth.

"They're from Spain."

"Ours are better," I said, although I wasn't sure I believed it.

He put me into bed.

I buried my face in the pillow. My leg felt heavy, and it was hard to turn from side to side. My father opened the tall wardrobe and poked around in the back of it. I didn't know what he was looking for, and he didn't take anything out. I could still taste the sweetness of the orange on my lips.

"Pa, were there ever circus performers in our family, or were we always citrus growers?"

He laughed. None of his ancestors had been farmers. They had been peddlers in Eastern Europe who had gone from village to village with a horse and wagon, selling things like laces and thread.

"You mean like Tova?" I asked, crestfallen.

He laughed again.

This village our family immigrated to was once very small. Five families were all it had in the beginning. None had the slightest idea how to grow anything. It was a struggle, and one family left, leaving only four. One of those was composed of my grandfather, my grandmother, and their little baby, who was my father. Another was headed by Arele Zussman's grandfather. My grandparents and the Zussmans were good friends. They weren't used to the Middle Eastern sun and sky yet. The stony earth hurt their feet. They had come from a land of snow, and Israel was a hot, rocky place, nothing at all like what they had imagined.

"Were they disappointed?" I asked.

"They hung on," said my father, rummaging in the wardrobe again. I noticed that he hadn't answered my question. Monsieur Maurice wasn't the only one. I looked out the window. All I could turn was my head. There were no lights in Monsieur Maurice's shop.

"It's a good thing they didn't give up," I said to the window.

My father finally found what he was looking for. He took out a blanket with a flower pattern and whispered that it had once been my mother's.

"Human beings can't migrate every year to a better climate," he said. "They're not wagtails."

"Sometimes they wish they were." I pulled the blanket up to my chin. One leg was cold and one wasn't.

"But they're not. They don't have a white bib."

"What do they have?" I felt my eyes shutting. The blanket smelled of orange marmalade.

"Black bibs," said my father, and he turned out the light.

seventeen

All the kids in the village wanted to draw on my cast. Suddenly I was as popular as if I really had flown. No one could figure out what I was doing in a tree top the day I fell. I kept mum, as they say, despite all the wild guesses. Baruch thought I must have been looking for old oranges. Mazal said I was counting the leaves on the branches. My teacher, who came to see me too, remembered my asking about wagtails and thought I must have been looking for their nests. In the end the village agreed that I had climbed the tree to tell everyone down below that rain was on its way.

Arele didn't try to guess. He didn't answer when he was asked how he had found me, either. I didn't tell the truth to anyone, and pretty soon it was all forgotten and I was left with a broken leg. At first the pain was so sharp and piercing that I had to lie without moving. The village's one and only doctor, who had been late to the clinic that day because he was delivering twins, came to have a look at me. He put his ear to the cast, tapped on it three times as if it were my skin, and asked if it hurt.

After a while the pain rubbed off on the cast, and I got used to the hard white casing beneath the blanket. I learned how to raise it like a crane and how to make a tent pole out of it. I also kept time to music on it to keep from being bored.

I lay in bed for a solid week. Tova came three times a day, and I got used to the racket she made with the pots and pans in the kitchen. She cooked the same thing each time, which made me wonder whether she was really the great chef she pretended to be. On the fourth day she surprised me with a box of bonbons, each wrapped in gold foil. She said they were her best chocolates and that she had been saving them for a special occasion, perhaps even for her wedding guests.

I had no appetite. The chocolate tasted bitter. Maybe it had gone bad from being kept too long. Tova showed me how to save the gold paper from the brown ball of chocolate without tearing it and to smooth it out again with a sharp fingernail.

She glanced at my bitten nails but made no comment, perhaps because I had a broken leg. While waiting for the soup to boil, she kept an eye on Monsieur Maurice's shop. She described each customer for me and told me if he brought one shoe or two. Now and then she said things like, "That Yitzhak never takes care of anything. This is the second time this week that his sole's come apart." When the Turkish barber appeared, she couldn't control her curiosity, because he didn't bring Monsieur Maurice so much as a shoelace.

I myself had only one shoe beneath my bed, a rather dusty and pathetic one. The other—my right shoe—stayed polished and almost new in the wardrobe. Whenever I got out of bed at night, I felt the left shoe waiting for me. I thought of what Monsieur Maurice had said about pairs of shoes being separated and wanted to comfort it that it wouldn't be for long. The one and only doctor in the village promised me that I would be up and about by the end of the winter. I asked Monsieur Maurice to draw something on my cast. I had left a special place for him, right beneath the knee. But he refused.

"I can't draw," he said. I knew he was right because of the cage on the back of my notebook. Still, I wanted a memento from my flying teacher.

"I can barely even fix shoes," said Monsieur Maurice.

I felt I had let him down. I was sure that if I had flown before breaking my leg, he would have been ready to illustrate the whole cast. I wondered what happened to a bird that broke its wing. I didn't think you could put a wing in a cast. The other birds simply flew on and left it behind. I shuddered. I wouldn't have wanted to be a wagtail with a broken wing, lying by myself beneath the cold drifts of winter until I died.

The flying Jews of Djerba left no one behind. Everyone knew they took turns carrying the door of the Temple and arrived safely with it despite their difficult journey.

My cast was covered with funny drawings. Whoever came to visit signed it or wrote the sort of thing you write in a class yearbook. I had a whole gallery of comical rabbits; cowboys and

Indians; a Snow White and the Seven Dwarfs, with an ugly-looking Queen that resembled Tova; birds with crooked wings (that was the fault of the cast, which wasn't straight itself); and a poem that ran the length of my leg and went:

Roses are red,
Violets are blue,
I just dropped my pencil
And can't write more to you.

Near my heel Arele had inscribed the names of all the fruits he would invent one day: citrusinas, lemorines, tangenellos, and even something called a "paradise fruit." When he was finished, he asked, "Tell me, what did you mean that time that you said . . ." He was stuttering badly. I waited. ". . . that you said that you could fly?"

I rubbed my cast and pretended to be busy with something, just like Monsieur Maurice when he didn't want to answer.

The only one in my class who didn't come to visit was Rina Neumann. Arele made me swear not to tell anyone that one day she came to his shack especially to ask how he had found me with my broken leg in the orange grove.

I saved the place beneath my knee for Monsieur Maurice, in case he changed his mind. I didn't care that he couldn't draw. There were lots of children in the village who couldn't draw either. Actually, none of the grown-ups in the village were interested in drawing on my cast, not even my father. Tova wanted to daub it with a few drops of nail polish, but I wouldn't let her. "No one draws with nail polish," I said covering my cast with the blanket.

"What's in that tall wardrobe?"

"Just a lot of clothes."

"Whose?"

"Ours."

"Your father still keeps your mother's . . . ?"

I didn't want to hear the end of the question. I wouldn't have told her even if I knew. I kicked the wardrobe door with my cast, and it banged shut at once.

eighteen

"Why doesn't Monsieur Havivel come to see you?" asked Tova with a show of innocence.

The potato pancakes she had made for me tasted burned, and I threw them in the garbage as soon as she left the kitchen. Anyway, Hanukkah was over.

I said that Monsieur Maurice was busy and added that some people had no time to waste because they had to work. When I asked who was minding her store while she puttered around in our kitchen, she gave me a mysterious look. Soon, she answered, she would have a partner to help her and would no longer have to spend all day on her feet.

I begged my father to tell her to stop coming, but he said that someone had to cook.

"Monsieur Maurice can bring me bread and olives. I like bread and olives."

"Monsieur Havivel is busy. He has a lot to do," said my father enigmatically.

I tried not to show how hurt I was. Monsieur Maurice had hardly come to see me. The door of his shop was shut for hours at a time. My cast was already gray with grime, and loose threads of gauze were sticking out from beneath it. The one and only nurse in our village came once a week to check up on me. Her little son held her scissors and kept asking when he could cut off the cast.

All the drawings and mementos were smudged, and it was hard to make out the ugly Queen. Arele's list of fruit was illegible. And still I went on saving a space for Monsieur Maurice beneath the knee. It was a small white island just for him, even though I felt he was avoiding me. A cloud seemed to have been hanging over him since the day I fell. When he crossed our yard to his shoe shop, he kept his eyes on the ground, as if he were embarrassed to look up. The circus, the elephants, the trapeze artists—all were a distant memory. I couldn't help thinking how overjoyed he would have been had I been able to fly. He would have had many more pupils, all coming to learn the secret that had belonged to King Solomon's great-grandchildren's   great-grandchildren's great-grandchildren.

I looked at my cast. It was as faded as old clothes. It wasn't even good for a hand-me-down, just for the garbage pail. I felt my leg inside it straining to get back its strength. It was ready to try again. Monsieur Maurice would train me, and this time I would wait patiently until he gave me the okay.

The day my cast was to be taken off, I saw two strangers step into Monsieur Maurice's shop. One held a briefcase and the other mopped his sweaty brow with a red handkerchief. It was strange to see someone perspiring from heat in the middle of the winter. I hopped out into the yard on my good foot. The two men weren't in the shop for long. I saw Monsieur Maurice sign a long sheet of paper and the man with the handkerchief shake his hand. Then he flipped his handkerchief in the air. It fluttered there for a moment like a crimson bird and landed on one finger. The man with the briefcase laughed. Monsieur Maurice didn't.

When they were gone, I knocked quietly on

the door and opened it. Monsieur Maurice was without his hammer and had no nails in his mouth. The shelves were nearly empty and held only a few pairs of shoes. The fancy slippers were back again, though. Perhaps I had only imagined that they were gone. Monsieur Maurice looked sadly at my broken leg and said nothing.

"I know who that man with the red handkerchief is. He's from the circus, isn't he?"

Monsieur Maurice moved his head slowly, but I wasn't sure what it meant. Was he from the circus or wasn't he?

"He can't fly," said Monsieur Maurice.

"But I will—you'll see! You were right. I wasn't ready. But next time I'll wait until I am."

"Maybe someday," he said, bending to pick up a few nails from the floor.

"You'll see. You all will. I'll be Israel's first flying trapeze artist."

He put the nails he had collected into a box on the table.

"How long does a circus last?" I asked. "Until the ringmaster is too old? Until the trapeze artists have wrinkles?"

"Some circuses go on for centuries. They're passed on from father to son and son to grandson. Their secrets are handed down too."

I knew the secret that had been handed down on Djerba. It was the secret of the flying Jews.

He touched my cast.

"Does it still hurt?" His voice was gentle.

I shifted my weight to my good leg. The cast suddenly felt heavy. I pointed to the island that I had saved beneath my knee, but he had already turned around and was taking down the white slippers from the top shelf.

"Maybe they'll fit you now."

I held one of them cautiously. I was afraid to touch it. It was the most beautiful thing I ever had seen. The tiny beads clicked as I slipped it onto my good foot. I stood in the middle of the shop, my right leg in its decrepit cast and my left foot in the mysterious slipper. It was too beautiful to step on the dirty ground with. A shoe like that was only for flying. I felt I was walking on air, the way I had the day that the rain came. I breathed deeply and felt the tree's leaves protecting me, as if I were a wagtail who lived in them.

"Will she ever come?" I asked hopefully.

Monsieur Maurice held the other shoe and stroked it gently with the same fingers that were so good at driving nails into soles. I told him I thought I heard footsteps outside, but he said that no one was there.

"A circus lasts until the people stop coming. Until no one cares anymore. The saddest thing is when a circus animal outlives its trainer. Do you know why the lion tamer never grows old and the trapeze artist never gets wrinkles? Because they die young. But the animals grow old and miss them."

I carefully took off the shoe. Once again I thought I heard someone in the yard.

"I'm sure she'll come back someday. You don't forget a pair of shoes you once flew in."

Monsieur Maurice returned them to the shelf.

"You don't need shoes to fly. Just keep your fingers to the ground. Think of the earth as a huge womb in which all kinds of roots and grubs are lying perfectly quietly. You're angry at the earth, but remember that in its womb are the flowers that will bloom in the spring after drinking up all the rain. And all the people we have loved and still love though they are dead. Remember that they are near you and holding you up. It's from them that you'll get the strength to fly."

I stared at the ground. Although the sun was shining in the window, I couldn't see a thing, not even Monsieur Maurice. I thought of my mother, who was buried in the cemetery at the end of the village. She was lying deep beneath the hard stones. She was the one and only dead mother in the village.

n i n e t e e n

Everybody first learns to fly in their sleep. I'm sure it was in mine that I took off from the ground for the first time. The trouble with most people is that they wake up in the morning and forget the night. They're still glued to the earth as if nothing had happened.

People—and not just in our village—are half like trees. That is, they have roots and they have branches, but their branches don't reach high enough for the blue to fade from the sky.

I can't remember when I first wanted to fly. And yet I so badly don't want to forget. I try not to, but I'm not sure it's possible. The fear of forgetting sometimes makes me want not to grow up. I can't even clearly picture my mother's face anymore.

I haven't forgotten Monsieur Maurice Havivel. I was never to see him again, although I didn't know it at the time.

I returned home to find the nurse waiting

for me with her scissors. She had come in the morning when her son was in nursery school, and he was sure to be disappointed. Tova was waiting with her, nervously wiping her hands on a stained apron.

"Where did you disappear to this time?" she grumbled, shaking a peeling nail at me. "Don't you think I don't know. Oh, you just wait, you just wait!"

The nurse asked me to stretch out my leg. I picked it up with my hands as if it were a heavy bolt of fabric and put it on a chair. The nurse snipped slowly and kept telling me not to move. Finally she split open the cast, and there was my new leg, like a butterfly emerged from a cocoon. It wasn't very different from the old one, just a little thinner and paler. But it was the one and only right leg I had in the village.

"Come on, try walking on it," said the nurse impatiently. Tova stood by her side. I had no idea why she looked so angry.

I bent down for a shoe, but the only shoe I could find beneath my bed was the one I had worn on my good foot all winter. Now I had to put it on the other one.

"You look like Charlie Chaplin," snickered Tova. The nurse couldn't keep from laughing.

I took a step.

For a moment the old pain stabbed through me, and then it ebbed slowly away. It was as worn out as the cast, which the nurse tossed away by the wall—an old, scribbled cast on which you could still see the smudge that had been Arele's list.

"Very good," said Tova, tightening her apron string. "Won't your father be surprised!"

"Stay well now, and don't go climbing any more trees. You're not a monkey," said the nurse, and left.

Tova wanted to throw the cast away, but I wouldn't let her. I picked it up and found Monsieur Maurice's white island beneath the knee. He never did draw on it. There was no need to step on my foot to feel the pain. The one and only thing our village didn't have was an artist.

A shiver ran up my bare foot from the cold floor. So the wagtail had rejoined the other birds after all. It hadn't frozen to death. Someone had taken care of it. Its broken wing would fly again when spring came.

When it came to flying, Monsieur Maurice had told me, there were no real teachers. He hadn't had any either. When life became too hard for the Jews of Djerba and they were about to be sent to their deaths, they flew. That was what he told me. Without circus tents and elephants. Those were his last words to me. I didn't want to contradict him, but though the Jews may have flown to Djerba after the destruction of the Temple, by the time they came back to Israel again, they had no wings. They did it on foot.

I gave the cast a hug. I don't know why, but I didn't want to part with it.

Tova went back to the kitchen to peel potatoes. Pots and pans were lying everywhere, and the cabinet doors were all open. She stood by the gas burners with her back to me.

"The earth, huh? So you'd like to know what's down there, would you?"

I took a step, realizing that Tova was the person I'd heard in the yard.

She turned around, holding out to me a large potato that was still streaked with mud.

"This is what's down there." Oil splattered in

the frying pan and kicked up little sizzles. Tova dried her hands on her apron and burst out laughing.

"The stories he tells you! I heard it all. So that's it! It was all his idea. You wanted to fly. Just wait until your father finds out. You're out of your mind, that's what! Circuses and flying Jews—whoever heard of such a thing? You should be ashamed of yourself. A big girl like you believing in the tall tales of an old shoe-maker!"

She had been in the yard, eavesdropping behind the door. My foot inched forward some more. It had its will power back again, and what it wanted to do was kick.

"He is not old! You're just as old as he is. And you burn all your pancakes. I'm not touching your food anymore."

She peeled the potato with quick move-ments and put it down on the counter, all white and naked. The knife was still in her hand.

"He wasn't even a real shoemaker. I know everything. I asked around. Do you know where he learned to fix shoes? In a Nazi concentration camp! Yes, they even got to Djerba—it's not the end of the world, you know, just a lump of earth in the ocean. When the German officers asked him what he could do, he said the first thing he thought of, because he was staring at their shiny boots."

I wanted to shove her away or pour the hot oil on her, but pain shot through my foot. I felt like a naked, peeled potato myself. I wanted my cast back for protection. Tova leaned the knife against the hot pan and stepped up to me.

"There was never any circus on Djerba. And no Jews ever flew there. Jews run, they don't fly. Believe me, I ran for my life too. Like a stray dog I ran. I know all there is to know about Monsieur Maurice Havivel. I wanted to marry him. He could have helped me in the store. But he already was married once. Maybe he even had children. That's one thing I never found out. And I've decided I could never marry a man who once loved someone else."

It was suddenly quiet in the kitchen. The frying pan was smoking. Tova had forgotten to add the pancakes and had burned the oil. She turned off the burner and told me to open the windows. I walked slowly over to them, feeling

how I limped and missing my doodled old cast.
When I opened the window that faced the shoe
shop, I heard her say, "I'll bet you don't even
know that he's sold out and left."

t w e n t y

He's not even a real shoemaker, I heard her
shouting in my dream. I tossed and turned. I
dreamed my leg was still in a cast. Finally I
ditched Tova and went somewhere else. I wasn't
sure where I was. I was surrounded by the
pounding of surf. All at once I realized I was on
an island. Someone told me to shut my eyes and
took my hand. I asked not to walk so fast,
because my leg was in a cast and I limped.
"Never mind," said the person, and, whenever
we came to a corner, told me to turn right or
left. Always right, and then left, like a pair of
shoes that stayed together. I said my bad leg was
barefoot. "Never mind," said the person. "We'll
keep off the thorns." And in fact I felt no pain
and nothing hurt when I stepped on it. My eyes
were shut tight. We came to a large house. I was
told to run my hand over the door, but even
before I touched it, I knew it belonged to the
wondrous synagogue of Djerba and came from

the Temple in Jerusalem. Although in my dream I was sure that my guide was Monsieur Maurice, I was surprised to see when I opened my eyes that it was a woman. It wasn't just any woman, either, but one dressed like a trapeze artist.

"Who are you?"

Her smile was warm and loving.

"Are you from Monsieur Maurice's circus?" I shouted excitedly in my dream.

"I'm more than that." Even in the dark I could see she had beautiful eyes.

"Do you come from Djerba?"

"And from the earth." When she turned her head, I saw that she had a very long braid that reached all the way to her ankles.

The sound of the surf was louder now. Either the waves were coming closer or the island was shrinking. The woman told me to touch the synagogue door and then ran a soft finger over my cheek, stretched out her arms, and took to the air. I saw she knew the secret and marveled at how beautifully she flew. I was sorry that Arele wasn't with me in my dream to see that it was possible to fly. I couldn't imitate her movements. How would I ever learn without

Monsieur Maurice? He wasn't even a real shoe-maker. I don't remember whether I shouted "Ma!" before waking up.

"Why are you screaming, Hadara? Does something hurt you?"

My father was kneeling by the side of my bed.

I flexed my knee. It was hard to believe that my cast was gone. In my dream it had been so real.

"He sold his shop and ran away. He's a coward, that Monsieur Maurice." I wanted to bury my face in the pillow.

My father sat on the floor at the foot of the bed.

"Not all circuses are real."

"How do you know?"

"Monsieur Havivel told me. In a real circus the elephant doesn't always curl his trunk when he's told, the trapeze artist sometimes misses, and the Jews can't fly."

"He never was in any circus at all."

"Don't be mad at him," said my father. I turned my face to the wall and tried to imagine a flying tent, but all I could see was the cold, empty wall.

"If it's not real, I don't want to hear about it."

"What's real is sometimes too painful. And what isn't, isn't always a lie."

"He's a liar," I blurted. "Monsieur Maurice Havivel never could fly and never could teach anyone to fly. Just look how I broke my leg."

My father touched my knee beneath the blanket at the exact point Monsieur Maurice had refused to draw on.

"But he did teach you something."

I turned back to the wall.

"He didn't teach me anything."

Deep down I knew that I was now the liar.

The rain drummed on the window. The pane was covered with drops. Some streaked quickly across it and others crawled slowly. My father rose from the floor and went to the window. He touched the glass, his finger tracing the path of the drops.

"Ma never cut her hair, did she?"

He turned around and looked at my braid on the pillow. It was coming apart.

"It rained the day your mother died. It was the end of a drought then too."

I got out of bed and stood next to him. The raindrops danced and drummed on the window.

"At the funeral we were ankle-deep in mud. We didn't even bring umbrellas. Ever since then, I don't like the first rain. It scares me." He hugged me and shivered.

The shoe shop stood across from us, shrouded in darkness so thick you couldn't have cut it with a knife. It surrounded us like a huge black cast.

I never did find out how the Jews flew to Djerba with the Temple door on their backs. That's a secret that's lost forever. Monsieur Maurice Havivel had been in a concentration camp fixing shoes for the Germans. On the back of my wagtail notebook he drew a special cage for people, a terrible place you couldn't escape from even with wings.

Havivel meant "beloved of God." I wonder why he was called that. It doesn't seem to me God loved him much.

Monsieur Maurice had dreamed of flying just

as I had. And had failed. But what he broke when he jumped was not his leg but his heart. And you couldn't put a heart in a cast.

I had called him a coward, but my father had been afraid too, and so had I. It wasn't true that Monsieur Maurice hadn't taught me anything. He had tried to teach me to fly with both feet on the ground.

twenty-one

"Gimpy"—that became my nickname in the village. Yet by the time the scorching summer came again, both my leg and Monsieur Maurice had been forgotten.

When summer ended and the tree-planting season began, Arele Zussman's father became the biggest citrus grower in the village. Arele went off to agricultural school. He stopped stuttering too.

Everyone came to see him off. We waited for the bus to pull out and kept waving until it was out of sight. Rina Neumann went about looking sad and said that our village would never be the same.

In our backyard, not far from Monsieur Maurice's old shop, I planted the baby tree that Arele had given me. The stock and the scion had already joined, and I told Arele that I would patiently wait seven years for them to bear fruit. He promised me that when they did, we would eat it together piece by piece.

The shoe shop was sold to a new immigrant from the Caucasus who was also an expert at shoeing horses. It took a long time for me to dare visit it. One day, though, when the sun was beating down, I stepped into it. It was cool and shadowy inside, and the shelves were full of shoes again. The milky slippers were gone, though. When I asked the new shoemaker about them, he shrugged and said that he was busy and had no time for kiddy talk. I wondered if their owner had come for them at the last minute. I hoped that at least the two slippers had stayed together.

Tova from the notions store married a barber. Although at first she didn't know which barber to choose, in the end she chose the Polish one. Anyone in the village could have told her that the Turkish one gave better haircuts, but she didn't ask. Even though the Turkish barber used green hair oil and trimmed the edges straight with a razor, she preferred the Polish one. Their wedding was held in the autumn, right before the tangerine harvest. She had stopped using red nail polish, because it was a color the Polish barber hated, and she had to cherish and obey him. The day before the wedding she came to ask my father for a bouquet of citrus flowers. She was disappointed to hear that citruses flowered only in the spring and declared that she had no intention of putting off her wedding until then.

Everyone danced at Tova's wedding. Our one and only doctor danced with our one and only nurse, and our one and only grocer danced with our one and only librarian. Even the shoemaker from the Caucasus came, although he remained a wallflower.

Tova didn't dance either. She said her high-heeled shoes were too tight, and her new husband told everyone that he was moving his barbershop to the back of her notions store so that the Turkish barber could have the citrus growers to himself. Tova spread out all the records from the old trunk she had brought from Rumania, and as she put some Gypsy music on the one and only phonograph in our village, she winked at me and shouted over all the heads:

"It's the circus!"

The music drowned out her words, and no one paid them any attention. Tova was so happy that she wouldn't have to stand all day on her feet anymore that I couldn't be mad at her. I said "Congratulations" in my sweetest voice and even shook her hand, though I still bit my nails and tried hiding my own hands when I could. Tova put her arm around the groom and promised me a free haircut. I said that my braid would keep growing together with me until it reached the floor. My father, who came up behind me just then, wrapped the tip of it around his wrist and pulled me onto the dance floor. "Your leg is all well," he said, and we danced.

Everything went whirling past me—the villagers, the village, the sky, even the groves and the wagtails. I'm flying, I shouted voicelessly, I'm flying at last!

My wardrobe-climbing days are over. I put my summer clothes away on the first day of autumn and my winter clothes away on the first day of spring. I have my own way of knowing when this is, because whenever the seasons change, my leg aches. It's a dull pain, not sharp anymore, but it will never go away.

Sometimes, on rainy nights, I awake to the drumming of drops on the windowpane. I grope for my slippers, slip both feet into them at once, go to open the window, take a deep breath of the clean air, and catch a glimpse of the shoe shop across our backyard, as wet and silent as the island of Djerba. The Temple door won't ever be returned, because no one builds temples in Israel anymore. Just new villages and housing projects for immigrants. The shop is blanketed by darkness, bundled up and waiting for the morning. And yet above it—right at the level of the treetops—Monsieur Maurice is flying, his mouth full of nails and a milky-white shoe on each hand.

Historical Note

Djerba is an island off the eastern coast of Tunisia. According to local legend, its ancient Jewish community dates back to sailors from King Solomon's fleets. Another legend relates that after the destruction of the Second Temple in Jerusalem in A.D. 70, the surviving priests came to Djerba with one of the Temple's doors. This they installed in the El-Ghariba Synagogue, which the people of Djerba considered a holy site.

During World War II, Tunisia was under Nazi occupation from November 1942 to May 7, 1943. Djerba, too, was occupied, and 4,000 Jews were sent from it to Nazi concentration camps in Europe.

Most of the surviving Jews of Djerba went to live in Israel after the Jewish state was established in 1948.